DRESSING UP
Pip's Truly Fashionable Tale

Written by Samantha Brown • Illustrated by Alexandra Motovilina

Blue Balloon Books
An Imprint of Ballast Books, LLC
www.blueballoonbooks.com
www.ballastbooks.com

Copyright © 2024 by Samantha Brown
Illustrations by Alexandra Motovilina

All rights reserved. No part of this book may be reproduced in any form or by any electronic or mechanical means, including information storage and retrieval systems, without permission in writing from the publisher, except by reviewers, who may quote brief passages in a review.

ISBN: 978-1-662202-02-2

Printed in Hong Kong

Published by Blue Balloon Books
www.blueballoonbooks.com

To my Pip:

From the moment you could crawl, you found your way into the enchanting world of my closet. There was no need to unveil the magic; somehow you already felt it.

This book is dedicated to you and every child whose heart falls in love with dressing up. May you always find adventure and self-confidence in your clothes.

Over my head,
I stretch my arms through.
Mommy helps me get dressed
in clothes special and new.

These clothes, they will take you
where you want to be.
They'll open doors wide,
just you wait and see.

You are so lovely, so funny and smart,
and just watch what happens when you dress the part.
Mommy teaches me all about style.
Special clothes can make anyone smile.

When you feel your best,
you can achieve it all.
You can jump higher, skip faster, and catch any ball.

Little, sweet outfits and pretty, fun dresses,
Mommy uses my comb to brush through my tresses.
These clothes will take me places far and wide.
When you dress your best, you have nothing to hide!

After my breakfast, we head out to stroll,
whether it's warm and sunny or icy and cold.
I take a quick nap and wake up to greet
all the new faces as we walk down the street.

We end up on Park where we sit to have lunch.
The basket of breadsticks makes a big CRUNCH!
The clinking of glasses rings in my ears
as I giggle and giggle for all to hear.

This little outfit transported me here.
It feels so unique. The magic is clear!
Where will we go next? I wonder and yawn,
then nap on the subway as we ride along.

You can be quirky, be special, be you
with every last detail right down to your shoe.
Pick out your favorite—red, pink, blue, or green—
and head out for the day. See and be seen!

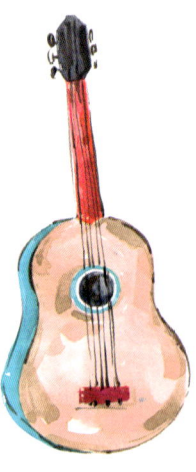

These clothes, they will take you
where you want to be.
They'll open doors wide,
just you wait and see.

I wake up again, and Mama speaks:
"My love, we are front row at fashion week!"
The models walk toward us and round to pass.
The photographers click, click, click and flash!

Fashion is where Mommy works every day.
Then, she rushes home to hug me and play.
I love the days when she takes me along.
I get so excited, I burst into song!

One more quick nap,
and my eyes open wide.
Is this real? It's the Met,
and we're going inside!

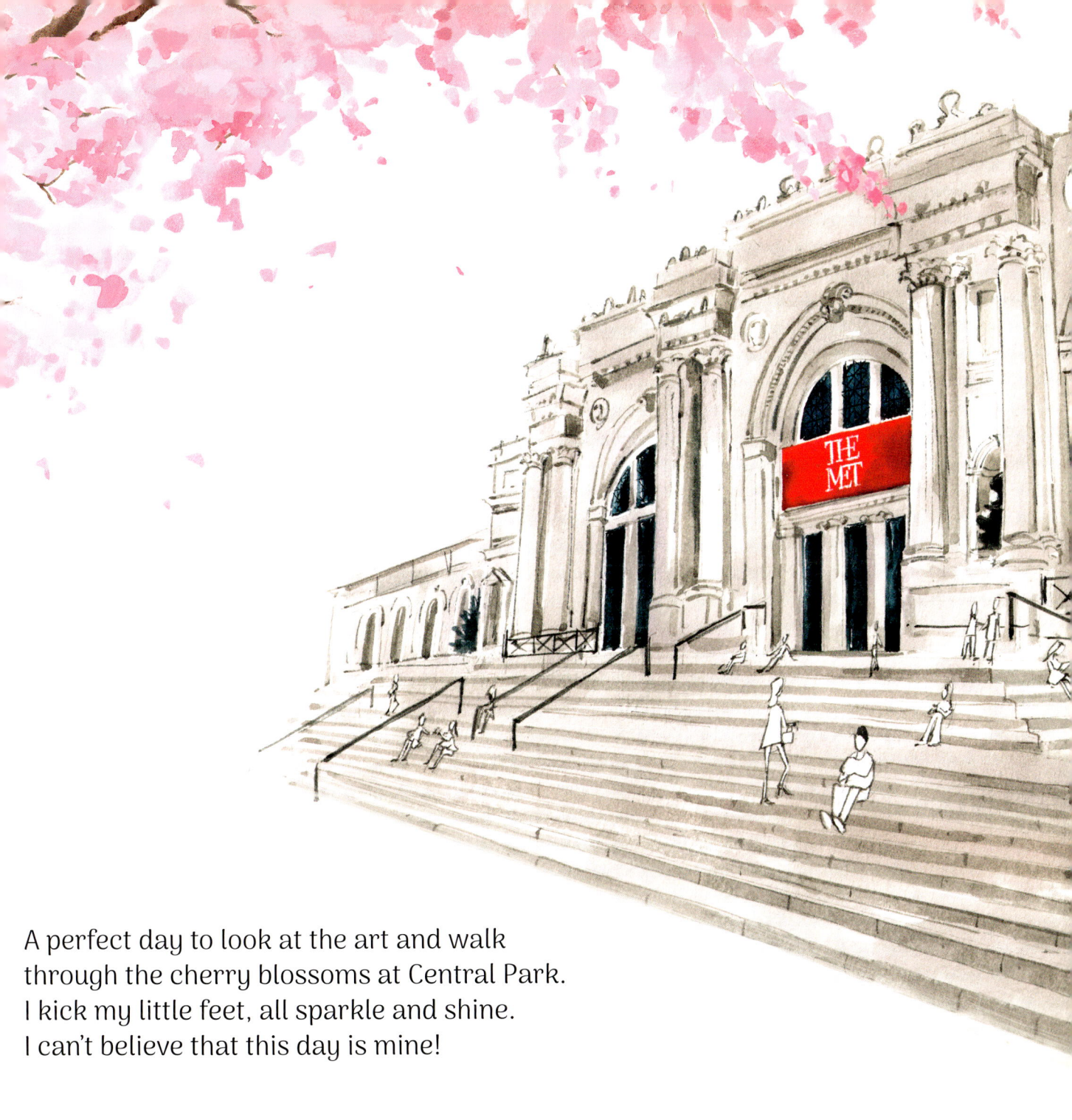

A perfect day to look at the art and walk
through the cherry blossoms at Central Park.
I kick my little feet, all sparkle and shine.
I can't believe that this day is mine!

The next day, I wake up, and there's a new dress.
Where will it take me? Where will I go next?
A quick little snooze, and poof—I'll be there.
I'm on an airplane, so high up in the air!

These clothes, they will take
you where you want to be.
They'll open doors wide,
just you wait and see.